Joke Book for Teen Girls

Teen Girl Gifts Trendy Stuff

Copyright © 2024

Welcome to the "Joke Book for Teen Girls"

But before you dive into these pages, let's set the record straight. This is not your typical joke book filled with tired knock-knock jokes or predictable "what did the" or "what do" setups. *No, this book is something different.*

Here, you'll find a collection of humor crafted specifically with you, the teen girl, in mind. These jokes are fresh, relatable, and designed to bring a smile to your face and maybe even a snort of laughter. Whether you're looking for a quick chuckle to brighten your day or a witty comeback to impress your friends, you'll find it here.

So, get ready to giggle, guffaw, and maybe even groan a little as you flip through these pages as a teen girl navigating the wild and wonderful world of adolescence. Enjoy!

Trying to pick an outfit for school like you're about to walk the red carpet, but end up wearing the same hoodie twice in a week. "Styling by: Laundry Schedule."

When you perfectly time your sleep to wake up without an alarm but then sleep through your backup alarms. "I was so close to being an adult."

The strategy involved in picking the right emoji. "This requires careful consideration."

What is an extreme sport? Searching for the right meme/gif to send in your group chat before somebody else says something and the subject changes.

The weird pride you feel when a baby stops crying because you made a funny face. "Call me the baby whisperer."

The personal victory of finishing a chapstick without losing it. "I deserve an award."

That moment you're trying to explain to your grandma how to use Snapchat filters, and she turns into a potato.

Finding an old diary and wondering how you ever survived that much drama. "Was I always this dramatic? Yes, yes, I was."

When you're too lazy to get the remote, so you just watch whatever's on. "Guess I'm into cooking shows now."

When you tell your crush you like their new post and they say "Thanks, you too" but you haven't posted anything in weeks. "Guess I'm invisible now, call me Casper."

Finding an old diary and wondering how you ever survived that much drama. "Was I always this dramatic? Yes, yes, I was."

The triumph of remembering your password on the first try. "I am the master of my digital domain."

When you found 6 good memes and decide to send to your bestie, and she replies with LOL to the last one! "No way, I want 6 separate replies cuz I can't send 6 good memes and you acknowledge one!"

The panic mode when you cook something new and accidentally create a new element on the periodic table. "Tonight, we dine on...science."

The awkwardness of saying goodbye and then walking in the same direction. "So, we meet again."

When your phone charger is frayed but find one good angle that'll make it charge, "I am HackerMan, with frayed chargers comes great responsibilities."

When you say "I'll just rest my eyes" during study time and wake up in a different century. "Time travel, but only forward."

When you find a long-lost item while looking for something else. "Today, I am an explorer."

When you try to flirt by laughing at your crush's jokes, but sound like a malfunctioning car engine. "And that, kids, is how I became single for life."

When you perfectly time your sleep to wake up without an alarm but then sleep through your backup alarms. "I was so close to being an adult."

When you finally clean your room and find that one missing item that sparked a household search party. "Found the lost relic of the Ancient Times."

The horror of accidentally sending a screenshot to the person you screenshotted. "Welcome to a new episode of : it's my world and you're all living in it without MILO MURPHY"

The gym selfie that's more about the outfit than the workout. "Sweating for the 'gram."

The delicate art of trying to plug in your charger in the dark. "A quest more challenging than finding Narnia."

Trying to make a TikTok dance video when your pet decides it's their time to shine. "Featuring: Fluffy, the real star."

Trying to quietly eat chips in a quiet room and feeling like a criminal. "Crunch quietly, crunch guiltily."

That moment when you open a test and reconsider if it's too late to become a circus performer instead. "Life under the big top can't be this hard, right?"

That moment when you and your best friend say the same thing at the same time, and you start wondering if you should start a psychic business. "We accept payment in pizza and good vibes."

When someone uses slang you don't know, and you're too afraid to ask. "Yes, that's totally...fetch?"

When you're about to take a bite, and someone says, "Can I have some?" "Sure, I didn't need happiness anyway."

When you're doing homework and your younger sibling asks for help with math. "Sorry, I only speak fluent TikTok."

Realizing you've been holding onto a pen but haven't written anything for hours. "This pen is my comfort object."

When you rehearse an entire conversation in your head and the other person doesn't follow the script. "Excuse me, you've got your lines wrong."

The struggle of trying to take a group selfie with friends, but it turns into an accidental documentary on why you're all still single. "Starring: Foreheads and double chins."

When you make a reference to a Vine, and someone asks, "What's Vine?" "Time to question my entire social circle."

The mystery of why you can never find the Tupperware lid that fits. "An unsolved case for the kitchen detectives."

Watching a Disney movie as a teen and realizing you relate more to the good guy. "Turns out, I too am dramatically misunderstood and have a flair for dramatic exits."

The silent victory of fitting into jeans you haven't worn in a year. "Guess who's the real 'fitspo' now?"

When you accidentally start watching a new show and finish the season in one night. "I guess sleep is for the weak."

That moment you realize your life is a series of, "I'll do it in 5 minutes," and suddenly it's midnight. "Procrastination? No, I call it time management... gone wild."

When you realize you've been pronouncing a word wrong your whole life. "So, it's not 'expresso'?"

That moment of silent panic when you can't remember if you locked the door. "Did I secure the fortress or leave it open for the trolls?"

When you're watching a romance movie and the characters finally kiss, but then your mom walks in. "Great timing, mom. Next, you' ll appear during my first kiss too?"

When your friend says, "Remember that time you..." and you're not sure what scandal is about to be unearthed. "Let' s not and say we did."

Trying to figure out if it's your turn to answer in a group conversation. "Jumping in... now? No? Okay, how about now?"

The face you make when someone says they don't use social media. "What do you mean you don't know what a meme is? Are you even from this planet?"

Trying to explain why you're laughing so hard at your phone, but you can't because memes are a language. "It's funny because it's true, okay?"

The illusion of productivity when you organize your study space but don't actually study. "Aesthetic productivity is still productivity, right?"

Trying to follow a makeup tutorial and ending up looking like a Picasso painting. "Abstract art or beauty guru, you decide."

The debate of whether it's too late for coffee. "It's never too late for coffee. Coffee is life."

When you're explaining something you thought you understood, and suddenly you don't. "And thus, the teacher becomes the student."

When you finally find the perfect spot in the library to study, but it's right next to someone eating the loudest chips ever. "This is not ASMR, this is a test of patience."

When you accidentally open the camera in an unflattering angle. "And today, we're exploring the potato angle."

The universal struggle of untangling earphones. "Today's episode: The Gordian Knot."

That one friend who's about to tell a secret but says, "Nevermind," and you're left wondering if you missed out on the gossip of the century. "Hello, FBI? I need a follow-up on a case."

The panic of liking a post while stalking someone's profile from years back. "Hands of steel, don' t fail me now."

Me: "Don' t double text, they still won' t reply" . Also Me: *Double texts and gets no reply. "Did I just play myself?"

When your WiFi stops working for exactly 1 minute and you're forced to get to know your surroundings. "Oh, so these are my parents. Nice."

Planning an outfit in your head, but it looks completely different in reality. "I'm telling you, it looked better in my head."

The stealth mode of retrieving a snack at night without waking anyone. "Operation Snack Retrieval is a go."

The panic of seeing "Read at 9:32 pm" with no reply by 9:33 pm. "Guess I'll start planning my life as a hermit now."

The moment you make eye contact with your friend in a situation where you shouldn't laugh, and it's game over. "Laughter level: Impossible to contain."

That awkward moment when your 'haha' turns into a snort in public. "I'm just practicing my animal calls, carry on."

Trying to diet, but you treat yourself every 5 minutes because you're proud you haven' t given up yet. "It' s a reward system, okay?"

When your dog hears you opening a food package from three rooms away. "Better than any home security system."

When you tell your pet a joke, and they walk away. "Tough crowd."

When you try to cook and the recipe says "chill in the fridge for an hour," and you're standing there wondering if it's talking about the food or you. "Both could use some chilling."

The struggle of trying to peel off a sheet mask gracefully. "I was going for serene, but I'll settle for not tearing it."

The paradox of "I have nothing to wear" in front of a full closet. "The great clothing conundrum."

That moment when you accidentally open the front camera and you're faced with the creature from the dark lagoon. "I was going for a mermaid look, promise."

Waiting for your favorite book to be adapted into a movie, only to realize they've changed everything. "This is why we can't have nice things."

When you're so tired, you start questioning your own existence. "To sleep, perchance to dream of being awake."

When you' re on a Zoom call, and your crush' s name lights up... because they're snoring. "Romance is not dead, just asleep."

When you try to use slang to seem cool but it backfires. "Yeet... Did I use that right?"

Trying to subtly use your phone in class and feeling like a secret agent. "Mission: Not Detected."

Planning to study with a friend and it quickly turns into a 5-hour therapy session about why fictional characters should be real. "I'm emotionally invested, it's serious."

The bizarre reality of explaining memes to someone who doesn't use the internet much. "It's funny because the cat is... you know what, never mind."

The suspense of watching two people type in a group chat at the same time. "Battle of the Typers."

The way you sprint to your room after turning off the lights downstairs, as if there's something chasing you. "Olympic record, here I come."

Deciding if you're too sick to go to school or just sick enough to miss that one class. "Strategic health planning."

The thrill of finding an extra fry at the bottom of the bag. "The little things."

When you finally clean your room and find that shirt you accused everyone of stealing. "Sorry for the false accusations, but it was a group bonding experience."

When your friend says, "Act natural," and you suddenly forget how to be a human. "Is this how I normally stand?"

When you plan to be early but still end up being late. "Time is an illusion."

Realizing you've been singing the wrong lyrics to your favorite song for years. "So you're telling me the song by China is NOT 'Tonight I'm a Soccer Ball?'"

The internal struggle of wanting to text someone but not wanting to text first. "To text, or not to text, that is the question."

That one aggressive key on the keyboard that always types in caps. "CALM DOWN, SHIFT KEY."

The art of pretending to study when really you're just aligning your pens in a color-coded symphony. "This is very important work, okay?"

The saga of finding the end of a tape roll. "A quest more challenging than any video game."

The saga of finding the end of the sticky tape. "A sticky situation."

Watching cooking shows and judging the chefs, while your dinner is a microwave meal. "Clearly, I have superior taste."

When your best friend tags you in a meme, and it's scarily accurate. "Are you spying on me?"

When you look at old photos and can't believe you let yourself out of the house like that. "A moment of silence for past fashion choices."

That moment you realize your pet has seen you do more weird dances than your TikTok followers ever will. "You're sworn to secrecy, Mr. Whiskers."

Trying to remember if you dreamt a conversation or it actually happened. "Did we talk about this, or was that my dream?"

The delicate operation of checking the time in class without making it look like you're bored. "Just admiring my watch, nothing to see here."

When you're trying to save money but end up treating yourself for being so good at saving money. "I deserve this, it's a cycle of financial self-care."

When you say you're going to have "just one more" snack and end up eating the whole package. "The snack that smiles back until you eat them all."

Trying to fit another book on your shelf like it's a game of Tetris. "A bibliophile's puzzle."

Trying to explain to your parents why you need a fancy dress for a school event. "It's not just a dress; it's my entrance into society."

The art of listening to someone while you're zoned out, and then they ask for your opinion. "Uh, can you repeat the part where you said all the things?"

When you need to sneeze as soon as you hide during hide and seek. "Bless me, for I have sneezed."

The dilemma of whether to charge your phone or keep lying in that one comfy position. "Guess I'll live on the edge... of battery life."

Trying to remember why you walked into a room. "Mission objective: Unknown."

The strange pride in giving good directions. "Yes, I am the human GPS."

When you wear a big hoodie and skinny jeans, and you look like a lollipop. "Fashion is about expressing your shape, and I'm feeling very 'round' today."

The mystery of socks disappearing in the laundry. "Socks: The ultimate escape artists."

When your pet looks at you like you're the weird one. "Judged by a creature that licks its own paws."

When your sibling uses all the hot water, and now you're contemplating whether they're necessary family members. "Survival of the warmest."

When you're watching a movie with your parents, and a love scene comes on. "Suddenly, I'm very interested in the pattern of this carpet

Deciding whether to keep a box because it's a 'good box.' "You never know when you'll need a sturdy box."

Trying to keep a serious face when your friend trips in public, because you're a good friend. "But we'll laugh about this... in approximately 5 minutes."

The awkward dance of trying to pass someone on a narrow sidewalk. "Shall we waltz or tango?"

When you're about to fall asleep, and your body does the fake fall thing. "Just practicing my ninja moves."

When you're asked to help with tech stuff because you're young, and suddenly you're IT support. "Have you tried turning it off and on? Yes? My expertise ends here."

That moment when your jam comes on, and your inner superstar is unleashed. "This is my moment, and I will shine."

The dance you do when trying to put on jeans straight from the dryer. "A workout in disguise."

The magic of finding an old gift card and not knowing if it's a treasure or just a piece of plastic. "It' s like a lottery ticket, but for shopping."

When you find a song that perfectly captures your mood, and it becomes your life's theme song for a week. "Repeat mode activated."

Trying to remember if you dreamed something or it happened in real life. "Alternate reality problems."

When you have a midnight snack and it turns into a full, three-course meal. "Welcome to my nocturnal diner."

The mini existential crisis when a website asks if you're a robot. "Maybe I've been a robot all along and didn't know it?"

The art of listening to someone's story while also trying to remember what you were going to say. "Multitasking, kind of."

The moment you realize your summer vacation plans are actually just a series of naps. "I'm an adventurer, but in the realm of dreams."

That moment of triumph when you correctly guess the Wi-Fi password on your first try. "I am the hacker they warned you about."

When you're the first person to like someone's post. "Early bird gets the... like?"

When you finally get the perfect selfie lighting, but it's in the weirdest spot. "Yes, I'm lying on the kitchen floor, what about it?"

When your perfectly planned hairstyle is defeated by wind the moment you step outside. "Nature 1, Hair 0."

The mystery of how your room gets messy again right after you clean it. "The Room Mess Monster strikes again."

The betrayal when your 'waterproof' mascara disagrees with the concept of water. "I was going for the panda look, obviously."

The challenge of eating a snack quietly in class and feeling like a ninja when you succeed. "Stealth level: Expert."

Trying to quietly unwrap candy in a quiet room. "Soundproof packaging doesn't exist, unfortunately."

That awkward moment when you wave back at someone who wasn't waving at you. "Just practicing my royal wave, folks."

The drama of choosing a filter for your photo that accurately represents the vibe you're going for. "Should I go for 'vintage aesthetic' or 'modern chic'?"

The panic alert of looking away from your screen during a video call. "They'll know I'm not paying attention."

The struggle of trying to quietly open a snack in a quiet room. "This packet is basically a public announcement system."

Trying to read your own handwriting and wondering if you were writing in ancient hieroglyphs. "I'm sure this was English when I wrote it."

When you finish an amazing book and have to return to the real world. "Book hangover."

When you and your friend say goodbye but keep walking in the same direction. "So, we meet again, for the first time for the last time."

The despair of watching your phone fall and doing that awkward grab in the air to save it. "Every time feels like the first time."

The irony of cleaning up before the cleaners come. "Pre-cleaning the cleaning."

Discovering a new series and realizing it's 8 seasons long. "So, I guess I have plans for the next 2 weeks."

When you rehearse an argument in your head and accidentally make facial expressions in public. "Yes, I'm fine, just having a heated debate with myself."

When you see an old email/username you made. "A relic from a less enlightened time."

The silent scream you do when you see a dog in public but can't pet it. "In my heart, we've already had a lifetime of walks."

The weird pride when your computer warns you a website might be dangerous, but you enter anyway. "Call me an internet explorer."

The silent joy of canceling plans. "Freedom!"

That one drawer that's basically a museum of past interests and random cables. "Here lies my fleeting hobbies and unidentified tech artifacts."

That moment when you're about to fall asleep, and you suddenly remember an embarrassing thing you did years ago. "Brain, why do we have to do this now?"

When you're not sure if you actually have free time or if you're just forgetting something. "Suspiciously quiet."

Trying to dance in the shower and realizing it's less 'music video' and more 'cautionary tale'. "Slippery when wet has never been more real."

When you finally decide to clean your room and find things you thought you'd lost forever. "So, this is where all my missing socks were hiding."

When your friend texts you "outside" and you're not ready. "Panic mode: Engaged."

The gourmet meal you make at 2 am because apparently, night-time is when you're a master chef. "Welcome to my midnight bistro."

The panic of sending an email and immediately worrying you sent it to the wrong person. "Let me just prepare my apology in advance."

The struggle of trying to drink water lying down without drowning. "Hydration or waterboarding?"

When your alarm goes off and you have to deal with the reality that you're not a millionaire who can sleep in. "Back to living my not-a-billionaire lifestyle."

The awkward silence after telling a joke and realizing you're the only one who finds it funny. "I'll just laugh at my own genius, it's fine."

Me reading message previews from the notification bar on my phone and not answering for the next 6 hours.

The internal debate about whether it's cold enough to justify not leaving your bed. "This bed is a self-sustaining ecosystem."

Trying to quietly open a can of soda in a quiet room and it sounding like a rocket launch. "We have lift-off."

The surprise when you accidentally take a great photo. "A masterpiece, if I do say so myself."

Realizing too late that your sarcastic text needed an "lol" to not sound mean. "Sarcasm, my old friend and foe."

When you make plans while in a good mood but regret it when the time comes. "Past me was too optimistic."

That one aggressive pedestrian button that doesn't seem to work any faster when you push it multiple times. "Button mashing: Urban edition."

When your earphones get caught on a door handle, and you're yanked back into reality. "Guess I'm not destined to leave this room."

The internal debate of whether to correct someone's grammar in a text. "To be, or not to be... that annoying."

The alarm of your own hair when you touch it in the water. "Sea giant or... just me."

The existential crisis of choosing a profile pic because it must say 'casual beauty' but also 'mysteriously intriguing.' "It's not vanity; it's branding."

That moment of panic when you can't feel your phone in your pocket because it's in your hand. "Modern problems require modern solutions."

The decision fatigue when choosing a movie to watch. "So many choices, yet nothing to watch."

When you have a great comeback but stutter it out. "And the Oscar for Best Dramatic Pause goes to..."

When you use a word you're not 100% sure about, and someone asks you to define it. "It's, uh, very... complex."

When you try to cook something new and it actually turns out well. "Call me chef."

The puzzle of fitting all your snacks into one microwave trip. "I'm not eating; I'm engineering."

Struggle of taking a group photo where everyone looks good at the same.The time. "Just one more, I promise."

When your comfort show starts feeling like a part of your family. "I've spent more time with these characters than actual people."

Trying to watch a 'quiet' video in public, and it suddenly screams. "Yes, everyone, I too am surprised by my volume control."

When you're typing furiously, and autocorrect decides to sabotage you. "Autocorrect, why must you turn my 'ducking' into something else?"

The confusion of waking up from a nap not knowing what year it is. "Time traveler, just woke up."

The suspicion that your pets have a secret life when you're not home. "I'll get to the bottom of this, Mr. Fluff."

The rush of nostalgia when an old song you used to love comes on. "Ah, the soundtrack of simpler times."

The internal struggle when you want to correct someone's grammar. "Grammar police, at your service."

When you're home alone and act like a contestant on a cooking show. "Today, we're making... whatever's left in the fridge."

When you confidently answer a question in class, and it's completely wrong. "I was just testing your knowledge."

The excitement of ordering something online and tracking it every five minutes. "Parcel Watch 2020."

The pride of using a big word correctly in a sentence. "Behold, my expansive lexicon!"

The bittersweet feeling of finishing a good series. "What do I do with my life now?"

When you're typing angrily, and autocorrect decides to betray you. "Not now, autocorrect!"

The secret hope that someone will chase you when you dramatically exit a room. "Cue dramatic music... now."

The pride of catching something mid-fall and feeling like a superhero. "Reflexes like a cat."

The satisfaction of peeling plastic off new electronics. "So shiny, so new."

When your friend starts drama, and you grab your snacks because you're here for the story, not the fight. "Continue, I'm listening."

Trying to walk past someone on the sidewalk, and you both step the same way. "Shall we dance?"

The strange feeling of seeing someone live their life who you only know from social media. "I know your life, but we've never met."

The art of taking a 'studying' selfie when really, you've done nothing but arrange your notes for the photo. "Productivity in its purest form."

The awkward moment when you're singing loudly with headphones on and don't realize how loud you are. "Live concert, sorry not sorry."

Trying to balance the hot and cold water in the shower. "A delicate temperature dance."

The quest to find the perfect spot in your room where the Wi-Fi works like it's not from the Stone Age. "A modern-day treasure hunt."

The awkward moment when you're singing loudly with headphones on and don't realize how loud you are. "Live concert, sorry not sorry."

When you use a word you just learned and feel like a genius. "Expanding the vocabulary, one word at a time."

When you buy something online and track the package every 5 minutes as if it's going to teleport to you. "On a journey, my parcel and I."

The confusion when you can't remember if you've already shampooed your hair in the shower. "To wash or not to wash again, that is the question."

The decision-making process of which alarm tone will be less annoying to wake up to. "Choosing the lesser of the so-wrongs."

Accidentally opening the front camera and realizing you've been a potato this whole time. "Potatoes have skin; I have skin. Therefore, I am a potato."

The victory of finding a comfortable sleeping position after tossing and turning for hours. "And now, I shall not move for the next 8 hours."

The moment of silence for a dropped food item. "Gone too soon."

The debate of whether to eat healthy or to treat yo' self. Spoiler: Treat yo' self wins. "A balanced diet is chocolate in both hands."

The silent scream you let out when you step on a Lego. "Floor is lava? No, floor is pain."

When you're not sure if you actually said something or just thought it. "Did I think it or speak it?"

When you're crafting the perfect playlist that nobody asked for but everyone needs. "DJ [Your Name], at your service."

When you finally clean your camera lens, and your selfies go from potato quality to HD. "Behold, the true me."

The internal pep talk before making a phone call. "You can do this. Just a simple call."

The horror of someone using your phone and you can't remember what's open. "Please don't judge my meme collection."

When you're about to do dishes, and someone adds more. "A betrayal of trust."

Trying to figure out the perfect temperature for sleeping. "Hot, cold, or arctic?"

The magic trick of turning a 5-minute break into a 3-hour social media deep dive. "I was on an expedition in the depths of Instagram."

The thrill of seeing your food coming at a restaurant, only to realize it's not yours. "The rollercoaster of dining out emotions."

When you find a comfortable spot in bed, but then have to get up to turn off the light. "Betrayed by my own comfort."

When you and your friends argue over where to eat until you're too hungry to go out. "Guess it' s a kitchen raid then."

Trying to be subtle while checking if you have food in your teeth. "Just a casual, totally not weird mouth check."

The mystery of how bags of chips are mostly air. "The great chip conspiracy."

The dilemma of whether to keep your room cold so you can bundle up or warm so you don't freeze when you get up. "Climate control, but make it personal."

The art of pretending to look busy when you see someone you want to avoid. "Ah yes, this blank piece of paper demands my immediate attention."

When you finally remember something that's been on the tip of your tongue all day. "Eureka moment!"

Trying to remember if you dreamt something or if it actually happened. "Inception: Teen Edition."

That moment of irrational panic when you flush the toilet at night. "Why does it sound like a giant awakening?"

The paradox of needing glasses to find your glasses. "A visually impaired quest."

The thrill of putting on a concert in your car, complete with dramatic hand movements and emotional expressions. "Car-aoke superstar, that's me."

When you attempt a Pinterest craft, and it ends up looking like a Pinterest fail. "I'm not crafty; I'm craft-adjacent."

The solo dance party when your favorite song comes on shuffle. "Dance like nobody's watching, because they're not."

When you finally find that song you've had stuck in your head but didn't know the lyrics or title. "It's like finding a piece of me."

The internal debate when an online form asks if you're a robot. "Do robots know they're robots? Am I sure I'm not one?"

The struggle of opening a package quietly during a meeting. "Stealth mode: Fail."

The strategic planning of walking past your crush multiple times, pretending it's a coincidence. "Oh, you again? What are the odds?"

When you spell a word so wrong that spell check has no suggestions. "I've invented a new language."

The excitement of a package delivery, even if you know what's inside. "Every delivery is like Christmas."

The joy of canceling plans you didn't want in the first place. "Sorry, I have a date with my bed."

The moment you confidently answer a question, and Google proves you wrong. "I stand corrected, and humbled, by the internet."

The betrayal when a pen stops working, but there's clearly ink left. "You had one job, pen."

The mystery of why we pack 17 outfits for a weekend trip. "I like to be prepared for any fashion emergency."

That feeling when you finally find a comfortable position in bed, but then you have to pee. "Nature's cruel joke."

The unexpected workout from trying to open a jar. "Who needs the gym?"

When you're quietly judging the drama while pretending to be above it. "I'm not getting involved, but please continue."

The detective work of figuring out whose hair is clogging the shower drain. "A mystery for the ages."

When you accidentally send a text about someone to that someone. "And now we play the waiting game."

That moment of silence before your favorite part of a song, so everyone knows it's about to go down. "Prepare yourselves, folks."

When you make a joke, and no one hears it, but someone else says it louder, and everyone laughs. "So we're playing it that way, huh?"

When your favorite song becomes popular, and you have to share it with the world. "I knew it before it was cool."

When you take a nap and wake up just in time to go back to bed. "I' ve mastered the sleep cycle."

Trying to drink water in the middle of the night without turning on the light and spilling it everywhere. "A nighttime adventure."

The art of dodging spoilers for a show you' re behind on. "No spoilers, please. You better work with me here."

When your Wi-Fi is so slow, you have time to ponder the mysteries of time between page loads. "Is the internet buffering, or is it just time telling me to go outside?"

When you see someone waving, wave back, and realize they were waving at someone behind you. "Just spreading some friendly vibes over here."

The dilemma of wanting to text someone but also not wanting to make the first move. "The texting standoff."

Trying to do a simple eyeliner look and ending up as a panda. "Went for 'cat-eye', ended up 'panda in the headlights'."

That mini heart attack when you lean too far back in your chair. "And that's enough adventure for today."

The challenge of not hitting 'snooze' on your alarm. "Just five more minutes..."

The confusion when you're about to sneeze, and it disappears. "Bless me? No? Okay, moving on."

The complex calculations you do to figure out the minimum amount of sleep you can get and still function. "If I sleep now, I'll have exactly 3 hours, 27 minutes, and 19 seconds of sleep."

The inner debate over whether to save or splurge. "Do I need it? Yes. No. Maybe?"

That moment you realize your 'temporary' storage place has become a permanent junk drawer. "Welcome to the museum of 'I might need it someday'."

When you're typing a rant, and the other person starts typing, so you stop to see what they say first. "Strategic communication."

Trying to remember all the passwords you' ve created. "Was this one with an exclamation mark or a number?"

When you're eating salad, trying to convince yourself, "This is delicious," but your heart whispers, "Pizza." "My brain says kale, but my heart says pepperoni."

The disbelief when you hear a noise at night and convince yourself it's the beginning of a horror movie. "This is it, the moment I've trained for by watching all those scary movies."

The excitement of finally understanding something you've been studying. "So that's what they meant!"

The mini dramatic pause when you can't feel your phone in your pocket. "It' s like everything just flashed before my eyes"

The struggle of trying to spread cold butter on bread. "Why must you turn this into a battle, butter?"

When you realize you' ve been watching tutorials instead of actually doing something. "I'm a professional watcher, not a doer."

Trying to remember someone's name mid-conversation, and your brain offers you every name but the right one. "Nice to see you, [Insert Correct Name Here]."

When you take a risk wearing white and successfully avoid spills all day. "Call me the spill ninja."

The mysterious disappearance of pens. "I had a dozen, and now they're gone."

The habit of checking the fridge every 10 minutes to see if new snacks have magically appeared. "Last checked: 1 minute ago. Status: Still no miracles."

The surprise when you find an old device and it still works. "Ah, ancient technology, you've served me well."

When you're hungry but don't know what you want to eat. "A culinary mystery."

The bravery of wearing white and trying not to spill anything on it. "Today, I am a warrior... against ketchup."

Trying to quietly eat something crunchy in a quiet environment. "Sound amplification mode: Engaged."

The frustration when you can't find a comfortable sleeping position. "Why can't I just fall asleep?"

That moment you're on a health kick, and someone offers you cake. "It's not cheating if the cake was a surprise, right?"

The dread of making phone calls to strangers. "Can I text you instead? No? Okay, I'll just rehearse for another hour."

When you think of a witty comeback too late. "I should have said that!"

When your friend texts "LOL" but you know they didn't laugh. "I demand a laugh receipt!"

That one drawer everyone has that's just full of random stuff. "Welcome to the drawer of forgotten things."

Deciding to clean your room and ending up playing with stuff you found from 5 years ago. "This isn't cleaning; it's time traveling."

When you can't decide if you're hungry or just bored. "A culinary conundrum."

When you're in a quiet place, and your stomach decides to sound like a dying whale. "Yes, that was me, and no, I'm not hungry."

The moment you start to question your existence while watching infomercials at 3 a.m. "Do I need a Snuggie? Am I living my best life?"

The awkward moment when you're talking about someone, and they walk in. "Speaking of the angel... I was just praising your... presence."

The panic when your favorite show ends on a cliffhanger. "How dare you play with my emotions like this?"

The surprise of finding money in your pocket from last winter's coat. "Who needs a job when you're a treasure hunter?"

When you finally get comfortable, and someone asks you to do something. "Why doth thou tempt me?"

When your headphones are in, and someone keeps trying to talk to you. "I'm in a very important meeting with my playlist."

The mystery of where all your bobby pins and hair ties go. "A Bermuda Triangle situation, but for hair accessories."

The dilemma of whether to go out or stay in and be a hermit. "To socialize or not to socialize, that is the question."

The awkwardness of holding a door for someone who's just a little too far away. "Now we both have to pretend this isn't awkward."

Accidentally calling your teacher "Mom" and questioning all your life choices up until that moment. "Can the floor swallow me now?"

The gamble of sneezing while brushing your teeth. "A risky maneuver."

Resisting the temptation of not looking when your friend is giving you the ultimate gossip about someone who is right behind you.
"Mission: Keep a Straight Face has failed."

When you laugh at a joke only you understand. "I'm my own best audience."

The struggle of trying to remember why you entered a room. "I knew I came here for something..."

The intense focus required to not trip while walking in front of a group. "Don't fall, don't fall."

Hey Darling, Just one more thing…

If you enjoyed this book,

Give us a smile by reviewing this book

Scan here to give us your review!

Want to enjoy more books or

free courses for your benefit?

Scan here for our Facebook page

You can also join our Whatsapp group,

for ladies just like you

Scan here for the Whatsapp group!

Printed in Dunstable, United Kingdom

65397929R00067